THE MOON, THE SUN, AND THE COYOTE

THE MOON, THE SUN, AND THE COYOTE

By Judith Cole
Illustrated by Cecile Schoberle

SIMON & SCHUSTER BOOKS FOR YOUNG READERS

Published by Simon & Schuster
New York • London • Toronto • Sydney • Tokyo • Singapore

SIMON & SCHUSTER BOOKS FOR YOUNG READERS
Simon & Schuster Building, Rockefeller Center, 1230 Avenue of the Americas, New York, New York 10020. Text
copyright © 1991 by Judith Cole. Illustrations copyright © 1991 by Cecile Schoberle. All rights reserved including the
right of reproduction in whole or in part in any form. SIMON & SCHUSTER BOOKS FOR YOUNG READERS
is a trademark of Simon & Schuster.

Designed by Lucille Chomowicz
Manufactured in the United States of America   10   9   8   7   6   5   4   3   2   1

Library of Congress Cataloging-in-Publication Data. Cole, Judith. The moon, the sun, and the coyote / by Judith
Cole ; illustrated by Cecile Schoberle.   p.   cm.   Summary: Coyote, caught in a dispute between the Sun and
the Moon, receives the gift of many improvements in his appearance but must ultimately be satisfied with
what he has.   [1. Coyotes—Fiction.   2. Sun—Fiction.   3. Moon—Fiction.]   I. Schoberle, Cecile, ill.   II. Title.
PZ7.C67348Mo   1990   [Fic]—dc20   89-29891   ISBN 0-671-69628-9

For my father, Martin J. Cole for everything forever
J.C.

Dedicated to M.M.Y.
C.S.

When the Earth was young, before people lived in the desert, the animals there could talk as we do. Then, as now, the Sun ruled over the day and the Moon ruled over the night.

The Sun worked hard all day and thought himself very important. The Moon, who worked hard all night, thought herself the more important of the two. The Sun was by nature hot tempered, and the Moon loved a good argument; so when they saw each other at dawn and dusk, they usually quarreled.

"Look at me," the Sun would say. "I am larger and more beautiful than you. You pale by comparison."

"Yes," the Moon would reply, "you are attractive in a brassy, obvious way. But my beauty is fine and delicate."

"Without me, the plants and animals would all perish,"
the Sun would say.

"That is true," the Moon would concede grudgingly, "but what
good is life without the rest and hope that moonlight offers?"

The Sun took credit for the seasons, the Moon took credit for the tides. And so it would go, each trying to outdo the other in importance.

One evening, in the middle of an argument, the Sun said, "Well, you must admit that the most beautiful animals are the animals of the day."

"Not a bit," protested the Moon. "Night animals are stunningly beautiful!"

"What about snails and centipedes?" sneered the Sun. "I suppose you think they're beautiful?"

Instead of answering the question directly (because secretly she thought the Sun might be right), the Moon said, "By your own words, they are alive only because of you."

The Sun grew very angry and flared. "Name me just one night animal that's as beautiful as Hawk or Mountain Lion, and I'll concede the point!"

The Moon did not have to think long. Although there were many beautiful night animals, she thought Coyote was the most beautiful. Coyote did not look then as he does today. His coat was fluffy, as silver as the Moon herself, and as soft as night mist. His eyes were large, round, and golden. In sleep, with his thin, little tail and his short, little legs tucked under him, and his tiny, round ears flattened back against his head, he looked very much like a little silver moon.

So when the Sun challenged her, the Moon didn't hesitate at all to say, "Coyote, of course, is every bit as beautiful as Hawk or Mountain Lion."

The Sun knew she was right and, growing quite red in the face, dropped immediately behind the mountains, creating a spectacular sunset.

The Moon thought the sunset very beautiful but would never admit it. "How vulgar!" she muttered, and rose amid delicate pastels before the sky could darken to its deepest blue. She was so delighted to have beaten the Sun in an argument that she boasted to Coyote about it.

"I've waited a long time to get the better of that hothead. Thanks to you, I have done it. From now on, there will be a special place in my heart just for you, and you will be my favorite. If you need anything, just call me and I will answer."

Coyote was very proud to be the Moon's favorite. For many days, life went along as always. At night, Coyote hunted for food. In the heat of the day, he slept under a shady mesquite tree.

One night, Coyote did not catch any animals to eat. The armadillos burrowed deeply into the ground. The jackrabbits ran faster than Coyote. Even the insects hid quickly out of sight. This was not the first time Coyote had gone hungry. Usually, his hunger drove him to hunt better the next night. But now he remembered the Moon's promise and he called out to her for help.

"What is it?" asked the Moon. "Why are you calling me?"

"I am hungry," howled Coyote. "I cannot run fast enough to catch anyone for dinner."

So the Moon gave Coyote long, strong legs that made him the fastest animal in the desert. Coyote caught all the food he wanted.

The Moon thought, "This is a good thing I have done. Now my Coyote is happy."

And, for a while, Coyote was happy. Then one night, a cloud covered the Moon. Coyote could not see well enough to catch anyone for dinner. He thought how easily the Moon had helped him before. And Coyote called again to the Moon.

"What is it?" asked the Moon. "Why are you unhappy?"

"I am hungry," howled Coyote. "I cannot see well enough to get my dinner."

So the Moon changed Coyote's large, golden eyes into small, sharp, yellow eyes. Coyote now had the keenest night vision of all the desert animals.

The Moon thought, "This is a good thing I have done. Now my Coyote is happy."

And, for a while, Coyote was happy. Then one cold night, when the Moon was very large and bright, and no clouds were in the sky, Coyote could not catch anyone for dinner. He howled his disappointment to the Moon.

"All the animals can see me in this bright light," complained Coyote. "What good is it to have the fastest legs and the keenest sight if my silver coat reflects your light like a mirror? I can't catch anyone for dinner."

Now, the Moon loved to see Coyote's silver coat reflect her light, and she did not really want to change it. But he was her favorite, and she had to admit that a shiny coat made sneaking up very difficult. She gave him a darker coat of mixed gray and yellow, so he could hide well in any kind of light. After that, Coyote could catch all the food he wanted, no matter how bright the night.

"This is a good thing I have done," thought the Moon. "Now my Coyote is happy."

And, for a while, Coyote was happy. But soon he began to think of more things to ask for. One day, while sleeping under the mesquite tree, he heard the songs of birds. That night, he called to the Moon again.

"If you give me a beautiful voice to howl with," he called, "I will be able to sing beautiful songs to you each night as you rise."

So she gave him a beautiful voice. Coyote asked for large, pointed ears, so he could hear other animals move in the dark. The Moon gave him large, pointed ears. He wanted sharper teeth, powerful jaws, and a keen sense of smell, and the Moon gave him those, too. He did not like his little tail, so the Moon gave him a bushy tail to match his coat. And each time the Moon helped Coyote, she thought, "This is a good thing I have done. Now my Coyote is happy." And each time, for a while, Coyote was happy.

Now Coyote was very proud of himself. He thought, "I am the fastest, strongest, most beautiful animal in the world. I am the best there is. The Moon is right to love me the most."

Then one spring day, as Coyote was sleeping under his tree, he was again awakened by the songs of birds. Coyote opened one eye.

"They sing well," he thought, "but I sing better."

He was just about to close his eye again when he noticed the scarlet feathers of a cardinal and the violet luster of a hummingbird. Plumed quail scurried by, and cactus flowers bloomed in delicate colors. Coyote became very jealous.

"The birds and the flowers of the day are more beautiful than I am," he thought angrily. "That is not fair."

He could hardly get to sleep again, he was so angry. Anxiously, he waited for night to come. Coyote did not sing a beautiful song to the Moon that night. As soon as the Moon appeared, Coyote howled at her.

"What is it now?" asked the Moon. "You are the fastest, strongest, and most beautiful of the night animals. You have the best ears, the best eyes, the most beautiful voice, and the long bushy tail you asked for. What can you possibly want now?"

"I have seen the birds and flowers of the day," said Coyote, "and they are more beautiful than I am. I thought I was the most beautiful, but I'm not. Make me look like the birds and the flowers."

The Moon grew pale with anger. "You are my favorite, Coyote, but you have become spoiled. I have given you everything you asked for, but you are never satisfied. This time you ask for too much. The Sun will laugh me out of the sky. He will say, 'Even the most beautiful of your animals wants to look like mine.' I'll never be able to show my face again. This time I will not give you what you ask for!" And the Moon covered her face with a wisp of cloud and turned away.

Coyote was indeed very spoiled by now and determined to have his way. He decided to ask the Sun for help. When day came, he called to the Sun.

"What do you want?" asked the Sun grumpily, for he remembered losing the argument to the Moon. Coyote told the Sun what he wanted. The Sun laughed. He was only too happy to help Coyote. In no time at all, Coyote was covered with feathers of every color. On his head was a quail's plume, surrounded by delicate cactus flowers. His tail was a mass of scarlet feathers and each paw a bouquet of tiny blossoms. Coyote ran to look at his reflection in the river.

"Now I am truly the best," he thought proudly, and only then did he curl up and sleep.

That night, for the first time in a long time, Coyote did not catch any dinner. Once again, all the animals of the night could see him from far away. They laughed so loudly at Coyote with his feathers and flower petals that they awakened every sleeping animal of the day. And every animal of the day laughed at him, too. Coyote slunk away in shame and misery. When the animals had stopped laughing and gone back to sleep or play, Coyote crept out and howled at the Moon. At first the Moon did not answer. Coyote howled louder and louder.

"Why are you calling me?" asked the Moon angrily. "You went to the Sun for what you wanted. And now you call to me?"

"You said I could call to you," answered Coyote. "You said I was your favorite. All the animals are laughing at me. I'm sorry I went to the Sun. Please help me."

The Moon almost left Coyote the way he was, but she didn't want the Sun to get the better of her. And she still cared for Coyote, in spite of his faults, for hadn't she made him the strongest and most beautiful of all her animals?

"Very well," said the Moon. "I will help you one last time. You may have back your thick, bushy coat and your long, bushy tail. You may keep your fast legs and your keen eyes and your sense of smell. You may keep your beautiful voice. You may keep your sharp, pointy teeth and your powerful jaws."

And the Moon thought, "This is a good thing I have done. Coyote has learned a lesson. Now he will be happy."

That morning, the Sun
and the Moon did not quarrel.
The Sun felt he had gotten even,

and the Moon felt she had
proved that Coyote preferred
being a night animal.

For a while, Coyote was happy. He sang to the Moon, but he did not ask for anything. Then one night, he thought, "Perhaps I asked for too much last time. If I could have just a few bright feathers, I would be happy." So he called to the Moon.

The Moon heard him call. "I have given you what you wanted," the Moon said, "but even now you are not satisfied. From now on, you will have to get along the way you are." And she slipped away behind a hill.

Since then, Coyote has hunted mostly by night, but also by day. He tries to get the attention of the Sun, but the Sun only laughs at him. He sings to the Moon, and she loves to listen; but when he calls to her for this or for that, she does not answer.

No matter how beautifully he sings or how loudly
he howls, Coyote must get along the way he is.

398.2   Cole, Judith
COL   the moon, the sun, and
          the coyote.